NUTS! NUTS! NUTS!

BEN LUCAS

SQUIRREL LIVED IN A LARGE TREE IN A LARGE WOOD.

ONE COLD MORNING, HE
SCAMPERED INTO HIS KITCHEN.
HE OPENED HIS NUT CUPBOARD
BUT IT WAS EMPTY.
HE OPENED HIS NUT JARS AND
THEY WERE EMPTY TOO.

HE EVEN OPENED HIS COOKER, FRIDGE AND WASHING MACHINE BUT NOT A SINGLE NUT ANYWHERE.

IT WAS THEN THAT HE NOTICED THE CALENDAR AND
THE BIG RED CIRCLE AROUND TODAY'S DATE.
THE MOST IMPORTANT DAY OF THE SQUIRREL YEAR.

IT WAS THE LAST DAY OF AUTUMN.
ON THIS DAY, EVERY SQUIRREL MADE SURE THEY
HAD ENOUGH FOOD TO SURVIVE THE WINTER.

"A CLEVER SQUIRREL DOESN'T DELAY, HE PUTS NUTS ASIDE FOR A RAINY DAY." HIS MUMMY ALWAYS SAID.

AND HE HAD NOTHING, NOT A SINGLE NUT.

SQUIRREL TRIED TO REMEMBER
ALL THE PLACES THAT YOU
COULD FIND FOOD.
HE RAN DOWN HIS TREE AND
RAN TO THE EDGE OF HIS WOOD
TO A LARGE BRICK WALL.

"I AM FINDING FOOD FOR THE WINTER AND THIS WALL IS WHERE YOU GET WALNUTS."

"YOU SILLY SQUIRREL," BADGER LAUGHED, "WALNUTS DON'T COME FROM WALLS." "YOU NEED TO GO AND FIND FOX, SHE HAS NUTS."

SQUIRREL RAN OFF FEELING VERY SILLY AND VERY HUNGRY.

"YOU SILLY SQUIRREL," CHUCKLED THE FOX, "I DON'T HAVE CASHEWS, I WAS SNEEZING."
"AAAACHOOO," SNEEZED FOX AGAIN.

"I NEED NUTS," WAILED THE SQUIRREL, "IT IS NEARLY WINTER."
"GO TO THE RANGERS HUT" SAID FOX, "HE HAS NUTS"

SQUIRREL RUSHED TO THE RANGERS HUT, FEELING VERY VERY HUNGRY AND VERY VERY SILLY.

INSIDE THE HUT HE COULD SEE A BATH, A SINK AND A TOILET, THEN HE REMEMBERED SOMETHING. LEAPING EXCITEDLY ONTO THE TOILET HE PEERED INTO THE BOWL. "NUTS" HE CRIED, "PEOPLE PEE IN THIS THING SO THIS MUST BE WHERE PEANUTS GROW".

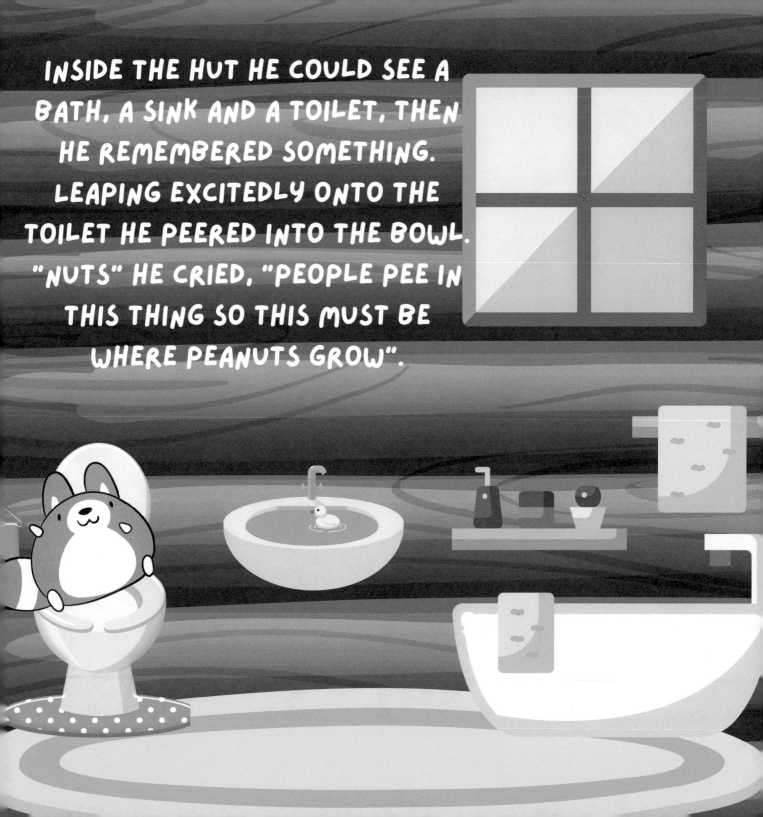

AS HE LEANED OVER HE LOST HIS BALANCE AND FELL HEADFIRST INTO THE TOILET.

SPLASH

SOAKING WET AND MISERABLE THE POOR SQUIRREL CRAWLED BACK TO HIS TREE. HIS TUMMY RUMBLED, HE FELT LIKE THE SILLIEST AND HUNGRIEST SQUIRREL IN THE WHOLE WORLD.

AS HE STOOD FEELING SORRY FOR
HIMSELF ANOTHER SQUIRREL WALKED IN.
"MUMMY SQUIRREL," HE CRIED, "MUMMY
IT IS THE LAST DAY OF AUTUMN AND I
HAVE NO FOOD, NOT A SINGLE NUT."

MUMMY SQUIRREL SMILED
KINDLY AT HER SON.
"I ALWAYS TOLD YOU TO PUT A
LITTLE BIT ASIDE WHEN THERE IS
PLENTY," SHE REMINDED HIM.
"YOU WOULDN'T HAVE MISSED
ONE NUT A DAY," SHE SAID.

"COME WITH ME," MUMMY SQUIRREL SAID.
THEY WALKED TOGETHER TO THE NUT
CUPBOARD.
THE CUPBOARD WAS STUFFED FROM TOP
TO BOTTOM WITH EVERY NUT THAT YOU
COULD IMAGINE.

SO WERE HIS NUT JARS, AND EVEN THE COOKER, FRIDGE AND WASHING MACHINE.

"OHHH MUMMY, I THOUGHT I HAD EATEN ENOUGH NUTS TO BE THE CLEVEREST SQUIRREL IN THE WORLD," HE SAID, LOOKING SADLY UP AT HER.

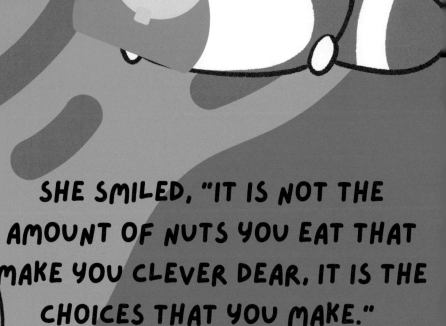

SHE SMILED, "IT IS NOT THE AMOUNT OF NUTS YOU EAT THAT MAKE YOU CLEVER DEAR, IT IS THE CHOICES THAT YOU MAKE."

CUDDLING UP TO HIS MUMMY, SQUIRREL SAID, "I HAVE THE CLEVEREST MUMMY IN THE WHOLE WORLD, WHAT'S FOR TEA?" "WHAT WOULD YOU LIKE MY DEAR?" SHE ASKED.

"NUTS! NUTS! NUTS!" HE YELLED.

Made in United States
Troutdale, OR
10/18/2023